HUFF 'N' PUFF

Written by
ALAN & SUZANNE OSMOND

Illustrated by
MACE WARNER

A TWICE UPON A TIME TALE™

The Three Little Pigs

Published by Ideals Children's Books
An imprint of Hambleton-Hill Publishing, Inc.
1501 County Hospital Road
Nashville, Tennessee 37218

Library of Congress Cataloging-in-Publication Data

Osmond, Alan.
Huff 'n' Puff / by Alan Osmond ; illustrated by Mace Warner.
p. cm. -- (Twice upon a time)
Summary: The three children of the little pig who built his house out of
bricks are threatened by the wolf and his son, who have modern tools at their disposal.
ISBN 1-57102-147-7 (hardcover)
[1. Characters in literature--Fiction. 2. Pigs--Fiction.
3. Wolves--Fiction.] I. Warner, Mace, ill. II. Title.
III. Title: Huff 'n' Puff. IV. Series: Osmond, Alan. Twice upon a time.

PZ7.O8345Hu   1999
[E]--dc21   98-48018
CIP
AC

First Edition

Written by Alan and Suzanne Osmond
Illustrated by Mace Warner

_____

Cover and book design LaughlinStudio

ALAN & SUZANNE OSMOND

Suzanne and I dedicate this book to our eight sons:

Michael, Nathan, Douglas, David, Scott, Jon, Alex,

and Tyler. . .a.k.a. The Osmonds—Second Generation.

When telling our boys bedtime stories, the concept

came that the classics can also live on for

a second generation and could be told not only once,

but "Twice Upon A Time."

MACE WARNER

These illustrations are dedicated to my wonderful Mother,

Mary, who early on decided it was in my best interest to

take art lessons rather than play ball with

my buddies on Saturday mornings.

Twice upon a time there was an Old Pig named Hank. Hank was that smart little pig who built his home out of bricks so long ago. Hank had two chubby sons called Oliver and Gus, as well as a roly-poly daughter named Sally.

Hank lived with Oliver in that very same brick house. Gus and Sally lived quite near in their own special houses. Now and then they would all get together for a game or two of checkers.

One day, as Oliver and Gus were halfway through their fourth checkers game of the afternoon and Sally was relaxing in the hammock with her new book, they heard a terrible racket of pig squeals.

Their father came running up the porch steps, yelling, "Oliver! Gus! Sally! That Old Bad Wolf and his boy, Fang, are up to their old tricks again. They are coming to get us and eat us for dinner!"

Checkers flew through the air as the brothers sprang to their feet. Sally's book landed in the bushes as she tumbled out of the hammock. They all ran inside and Oliver bolted the door.

"I can't believe this is happening again!" cried Hank, who was hiding behind the curtains.

Oliver, the biggest pig, squeezed his way into a chair at the kitchen table and said, "I'm sure glad that we still have this sturdy brick house to keep us safe. Those awful wolves can't get in here!"

Gus, who was slightly smaller, said, "And I'm sure glad that I built my new house out of steel! With all the wolf trouble these days, you can never be too careful."

Sally, the smallest of the three, said, "I was so worried about having a safe place to live, I built my new house out of armored tanks. It even has a big cannon. If I have any trouble with those wolves, they can huff and puff all they want, but this time, I'll blow *them* away!"

They waited to see if the wolves were coming, but there was no sign of Fang or his father, so Sally and Gus went home to their own very safe houses.

A while later, Hank was peeking through the biggest pig-sized peephole in the door of the brick house when he suddenly began to squeal. "Oliver! Oliver! I see them coming up over the hill!"

"Don't worry, Dad," said Oliver. "The door is locked, and there is even a pot of hot water on the fire in case they try to come down the chimney. There is no way those wolves can get us."

Outside, the Old Bad Wolf was setting up a jackhammer along the bottom of Hank's house. Fang stuck his nose right up to the peephole and growled, "Little pig, little pig, let us come in!"

"Just try huffin' and puffin' that hot air again!" Oliver taunted from behind the door.

"No huff and no puff," the wolf said with a frown. "This hammer will bring that silly house down!"

So they banged and they clanged 'til they tore the house down!

Oliver and Hank ran out the back door just in time. They ran as fast as their little pig legs could carry them, and soon they were pounding on the door of the house made of steel. Gus let them in, and then quickly bolted the door and turned on the security alarm.

Suddenly, the alarm went off. WHEEE! WHEEEE! WHEEE! Hank covered his ears and ran to the door. Peeking out the slightly smaller pig-sized peephole in the steel door, he began to squeal. "Oliver! Gus! They're coming across the field right now!"

"Don't worry, Dad," said Gus. "This house is made of solid steel. There is no way that hammer can knock down *my* house!"

Outside, the Old Bad Wolf was setting up a big metal grinder in front of the house. Fang stuck his nose right up to the peephole and snarled, "Little pig, little pig, let us come in!"

"Just try huffin' and puffin' that hot air again!" said Gus with a laugh.

"No huff and no puff," the wolf said with a frown. "This grinder will bring that silly house down."

So they wound and they ground 'til they tore the house down!

17

L uckily, Hank, Oliver, and Gus made it out the back door just in time, running as fast as their little pig legs could carry them. They were soon banging on the door of Sally's house. It was made of armored tanks and looked very strange. Sally had to use all her smallest pig strength to close the armored tank door after everyone was safely inside.

Fang and his dad stood looking at the strange house. "What a funny looking house you have here, Miss Little Pig. It's almost as funny looking as you!" roared Fang as he and his dad pulled out two huge cutting torches and put on their goggles.

21

"This is ridiculous!" shouted Oliver as he watched the wolves through the window.

"When will those silly wolves learn that they can't outfox us swine?" laughed Sally.

Just then Fang stuck his nose right up to the peephole and shouted, "Little pig, little pig, let us come in!"

"Just try huffin' and puffin' that hot air again!" yelled Sally with a grin.

"No huff and no puff," the wolf said with a frown. "This blowtorch will bring that silly house down."

So they torched and they scorched...and they scorched and they torched...but they couldn't tear *this* house down!

"Why don't we fool them and crawl into the house through the opening of that cannon? I once got into the old pig's house by crawling down the chimney," whispered the Old Bad Wolf to his son.

"I don't know, Dad. That doesn't sound like such a good idea to me. Maybe we should just call it a day," said Fang, who was getting kind of tired.

"Call it a day? Why, no wolf I know would give up when he's so close!"

"But Dad, didn't you say you landed in a pot of hot water when you climbed down that old pig's chimney?"

"Well, there isn't going to be a pot of hot water at the bottom of a cannon, is there, son?"

"I guess not."

The Old Bad Wolf gave Fang a boost and they began crawling down the barrel of the cannon.

H|ank, who was peeking through the smallest pig-sized peephole in the armored tank door, saw what was happening. "Sally! Sally! They're coming in through the cannon!"

"Perfect!" said Sally with a big smile on her face. "Don't worry, Dad. I won't let them touch a hair on your chinny-chin-chin. It's time we taught those bad wolves a lesson. Stand back!"

"Let's huff...," said Oliver as he lifted the cannon ball.

"And puff...," said Gus as they shoved it into the cannon.

"And blow those wolves away!" shouted Sally as she lit the fuse.

The pigs opened the armored tank door just as the cannon let out a terrific BOOM! They watched as Fang and his dad sailed high over the hill and disappeared. Later, Sally invited her father to stay with her as she helped her brothers build their own houses out of armored tanks. The whole pig family would now be safe if any more big bad wolves moved into their neighborhood.

As for Fang and his dad, they landed right in the middle of the county jail.

"Ow," said the Old Bad Wolf, rubbing his head.

Fang looked at his dad and shook his head. "Just great, Dad. Now we're *really* in hot water, just like you were once upon a time."

THE END